This book belongs to:

_____

_____

_____

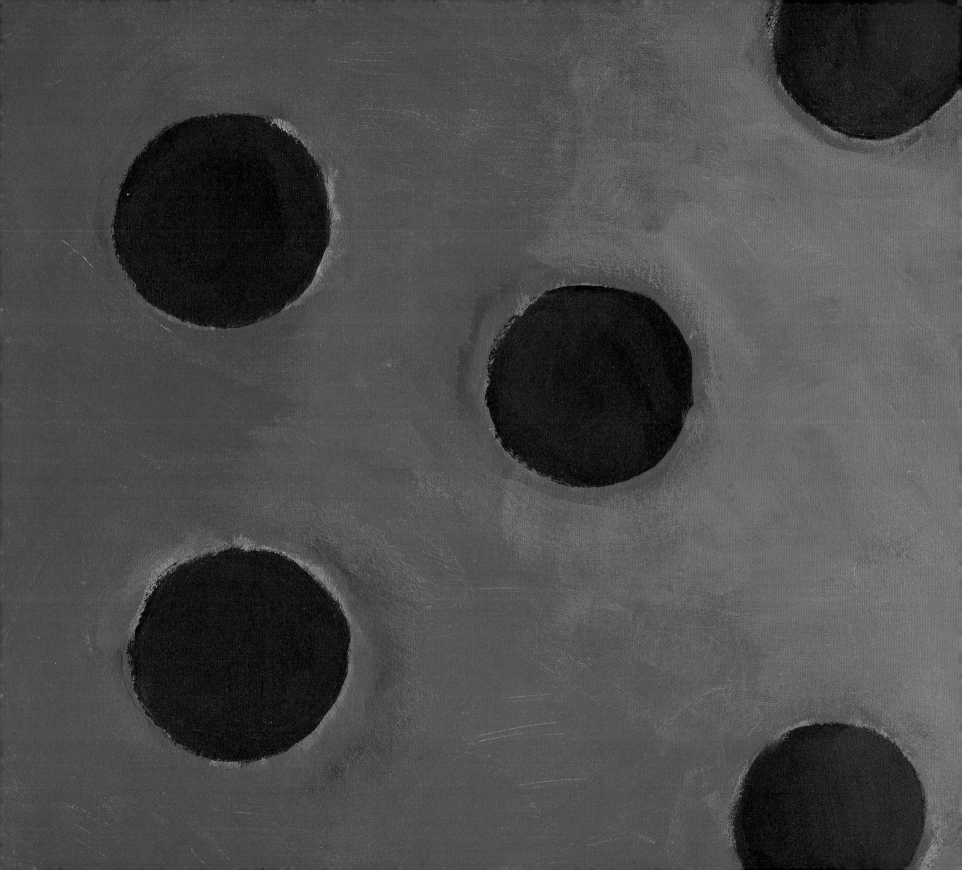

For Andrea & Claudia
— I.F.

For Mum & Dad, who helped
— J.T.

LITTLE TIGER PRESS
An imprint of Magi Publications
1 The Coda Centre, 189 Munster Road, London SW6 6AW
www.littletigerpress.com

First published in Great Britain 1999
This edition published 2010

Please note: The audio CD supplied with this book is
recorded by English theatrical artists therefore some words
will reflect the different dialect, for example ladybird = ladybug.

Printed in China
LTP/1800/0060/0110

2 4 6 8 10 9 7 5 3 1

The Very Lazy Ladybug

by
Isobel Finn

Illustrated by
Jack Tickle

This is the story of
a very lazy ladybug.

She liked to sleep all day . . .

And because she slept
all day and all night,
this lazy ladybug didn't
know how to fly.

One day the lazy ladybug wanted to sleep somewhere else. But what could she do if she couldn't fly?

Then the lazy ladybug had a very good idea.

When a kangaroo bounded by . . .

she hopped into her pouch.

But the kangaroo liked to

JUMP!

"I can't sleep in here,"
cried the lazy ladybug.
"It's far too bumpy."

so when a tiger padded by . . .

But the tiger liked to

ROAR!

"I can't sleep here," said the lazy ladybug. "It's far too noisy."

So when a crocodile swam by . . .

she hopped onto his tail.

But the crocodile liked to

SWISH

his tail in the water.

"I can't sleep here," said the lazy ladybug. "I'll fall into the river!"

So when a monkey swung by . . .

she hopped onto her head.

But the monkey liked to

SWING

from branch to branch.

"I can't sleep here,"
said the lazy ladybug.
"I'm feeling dizzy."

So when a bear ambled by . . .

she hopped onto his ear.

But the bear
liked to
SCRATCH!

"I can't sleep here,"
said the lazy ladybug.
"He'll never sit still."

So when a tortoise plodded by . . .

she hopped onto her shell.

But the tortoise liked to
SNOOZE
in the sun.
"I can't sleep here,"
said the lazy ladybug.
"It's far too hot."

So when an elephant trundled by . . .

But at that very moment . . .

the elephant

had to fly at last!